The Boxcar Children Mysteries

The Mystery in New York
The Gymnastics Mystery
The Poison Frog Mystery
The Mystery of the Empty Safe
The Home Run Mystery
The Great Bicycle Race Mystery
The Mystery of the Wild Ponies
The Mystery in the Computer Game
The Honeybee Mystery
The Mystery at the Crooked House
The Hockey Mystery
The Mystery of the Midnight Dog
The Mystery of the Screech Owl
The Summer Camp Mystery
The Copycat Mystery
The Haunted Clock Tower Mystery
The Mystery of the Tiger's Eye
The Disappearing Staircase Mystery
The Mystery on Blizzard Mountain
The Mystery of the Spider's Clue
The Candy Factory Mystery
The Mystery of the Mummy's Curse
The Mystery of the Star Ruby
The Stuffed Bear Mystery
The Mystery of Alligator Swamp
The Mystery at Skeleton Point
The Tattletale Mystery
The Comic Book Mystery
The Great Shark Mystery
The Ice Cream Mystery
The Midnight Mystery
The Mystery in the Fortune Cookie
The Black Widow Spider Mystery
The Radio Mystery
The Mystery of the Runaway Ghost
The Finders Keepers Mystery
The Mystery of the Haunted Boxcar
The Clue in the Corn Maze
The Ghost of the Chattering Bones
The Sword of the Silver Knight
The Game Store Mystery
The Mystery of the Orphan Train
The Vanishing Passenger

The Giant Yo-Yo Mystery
The Creature in Ogopogo Lake
The Rock 'n' Roll Mystery
The Secret of the Mask
The Seattle Puzzle
The Ghost in the First Row
The Box That Watch Found
A Horse Named Dragon
The Great Detective Race
The Ghost at the Drive-In Movie
The Mystery of the Traveling Tomatoes
The Spy Game
The Dog-Gone Mystery
The Vampire Mystery
Superstar Watch
The Spy in the Bleachers
The Amazing Mystery Show
The Pumpkin Head Mystery
The Cupcake Caper
The Clue in the Recycling Bin
Monkey Trouble
The Zombie Project
The Great Turkey Heist
The Garden Thief
The Boardwalk Mystery
The Mystery of the Fallen Treasure
The Return of the Graveyard Ghost
The Mystery of the Stolen Snowboard
The Mystery of the Wild West Bandit
The Mystery of the Grinning Gargoyle
The Mystery of the Soccer Snitch
The Mystery of the Missing Pop Idol
The Mystery of the Stolen Dinosaur Bones
The Mystery at the Calgary Stampede
The Sleepy Hollow Mystery
The Legend of the Irish Castle
The Celebrity Cat Caper

Warner, Gertrude Chandler, ,1890
Mystery of the stolen music

1995
33305239860756
mi   12/18/17

THE MYSTERY OF THE
STOLEN MUSIC

created by
GERTRUDE CHANDLER WARNER

Illustrated by Charles Tang

Albert Whitman & Company
Chicago, Illinois

Copyright © 1995 by Albert Whitman & Company

ISBN 978-0-8075-5416-6

All rights reserved. No part of this book may be reproduced or transmitted in
any form or by any means, electronic or mechanical, including photocopying,
recording, or by any information storage and retrieval system, without
permission in writing from the publisher.

THE BOXCAR CHILDREN® is a registered
trademark of Albert Whitman & Company.

Printed in the United States of America
17 16 15 14 13 LB 20 19 18 17 16

Illustrated by Charles Tang

For more information about Albert Whitman & Company,
visit our web site at www.albertwhitman.com.

Contents

CHAPTER 1

Getting Ready

"Are we ready or not?!" six-year-old Benny asked eagerly as he danced around the kitchen.

The Aldens' dog, Watch, awoke from his nap and barked excitedly.

Benny's older sister, Jessie, was making small round sandwiches. "Be patient, Benny," she said. She was twelve years old.

"I don't want to be late," Benny explained. "It isn't every day a famous orchestra comes to town."

"That's for sure," Jessie said. "Greenfield

is a small town. Usually, orchestras tour big cities."

Benny hadn't thought about that before. "Why *are* they coming here?" he asked.

"The Civic Center is a good place for them to play," their fourteen-year-old brother, Henry, answered. "People will come from all over the area to hear them."

"But they're not only going to perform," Jessie reminded him. "They've set up all those workshops to teach people about music, too."

"The conductor lived here when he was a boy," Violet added. She was ten years old and loved music. She played the violin and had been reading everything she could about the orchestra. "It was in Greenfield that the conductor first became interested in music. He wants to share his love for music with the people here."

All this talk about the orchestra made Benny even more excited. "Could we *please* hurry?" he urged.

Henry poured punch into a gallon jug.

"We won't be late, Benny," he said. "Besides, the reception can't start without us — we're bringing the food."

"And the decorations," Violet added. She stepped back from the kitchen table to look at the centerpiece she had made. Cardboard musical instruments circled colorful spring flowers. "There," she said. "It's finished."

"It's beautiful!" Jessie said. "You did a great job, Violet."

"I cut out some of the instruments," Benny reminded them.

"You were very helpful," Violet told him.

"Not helpful enough," Benny said, "or we'd be ready to go."

Henry laughed. "You can help me," he said.

Benny pulled a stool over to the counter and climbed on top. "What do you want me to do?"

"Put the tops on the jugs when I've filled them," Henry told him.

Benny nodded and set to work. When he had screwed on the last top, he jumped down from the stool. "Now what can I do?"

"I'd ask you to put the sandwiches in the boxes," Jessie teased, "but I'm afraid you'd eat them all."

Benny turned up his nose. "Cucumber sandwiches?" Even though they weren't his favorite, he took one and popped it into his mouth.

"Stop that," Jessie said, "or I'll have to make more and we'll be late."

"Is that the only kind you made?" Benny asked.

"No. There are other kinds," Jessie told him, "but they're all packed."

Benny looked in the boxes. Sandwiches of all kinds and shapes were stacked inside. They were all small. "I like big sandwiches," he said.

Jessie began putting the lids on the boxes. "These are tea sandwiches," she said, "to serve at afternoon parties."

"They look pretty on the plates," Violet added.

"I don't care how they look," Benny said. "Just so they taste good."

Everyone laughed. They knew how much Benny liked to eat.

"That does it," Jessie said as she covered the last box.

"So what are we waiting for?" Benny asked.

"Grandfather," Henry answered.

Mr. Alden had gone to pick up Soo Lee. The Aldens' cousins, Joe and Alice, had adopted her from an orphanage in Korea. The Aldens were orphans, too. They had lived alone in a boxcar until their grandfather had found them and taken them in. They were very happy living with him.

Just then, Grandfather Alden came in from outside. Seven-year-old Soo Lee was with him.

"You look pretty, Soo Lee," Violet said to the girl. She was wearing a pale lavender dress with a purple sash. "Those are my favorite colors."

Soo Lee smiled. "I like these colors, too," she said.

"Are we ready?" Mr. Alden asked. "We don't want to be late."

"Wait a minute," Benny said. "The cookies! Soo Lee, where are the cookies?!"

They had spent the previous afternoon baking at Soo Lee's house. Benny did not want to forget the cookies.

"They are in the car," Soo Lee told him.

"Great!" Benny ran to hold the door open. "Let's go," he said.

The others gathered up the boxes and jugs and ran out. Watch stood looking after them.

"We'll be home soon," Jessie told him.

He wagged his tail and went back to lie down on his rug.

Once the boxes were stacked in the back of the station wagon, the Aldens climbed inside.

"Off to the Civic Center," Mr. Alden said as he headed out the driveway.

Violet sighed. She had been looking forward to meeting the musicians — especially the violinists. Secretly, she hoped one of them would ask to hear her play. She had been practicing extra hours just in case. "I am so nervous," she said.

"Think of it as being *excited*, not *nervous*," Mr. Alden told her.

Violet laughed. "Well then, I am *very* excited," she said.

"Me, too," each of the other Aldens agreed.

CHAPTER 2

The Party

The Civic Center was buzzing with activity. People ran this way and that checking on last-minute details. A long table was set up in the reception hall. Arms full, the Aldens headed toward it.

"The orchestra has arrived at the hotel!" someone said.

"Hurry!" Benny urged. "They'll be here soon!"

Henry and Jessie spread a long white cloth over the table. Then, Violet placed her centerpiece. Henry poured the punch he had made into two large bowls. Soo Lee and Benny arranged the cookies on plates. Jessie put out the sandwiches.

They had just finished when Mr. Alden walked up. "Here's someone I'd like you to meet," he said. He turned to the young woman at his side. "This is orchestra member Melody Carmody."

Benny repeated her name silently. It had a musical sound.

She had curly red hair and a warm smile, and was wearing a pretty blue dress. "I'm happy to meet you," she said and put out her hand.

"Melody?" Benny asked as he shook her hand.

"Yes," she answered.

"That's a good name for a musician," he said.

She laughed. Even her laugh was musical. "I come from a musical family," she explained.

"What instrument do you play?" Violet asked.

"Violin."

"*First* violin," Mr. Alden added.

Violet's eyes grew big. She was talking to the most important violinist in the orchestra.

"Violet plays violin, too," Benny said. "Our cousin Joe taught her. Soo Lee here is his daughter. He's teaching her to play now."

Melody looked at Violet and Soo Lee. "Perhaps you'd play for me while I'm here," she said.

Soo Lee shook her head. "I'm just learning," she said.

"Next time, then," Melody said. "How about you, Violet?"

Violet sputtered. "Oh, I — "

"She's *good*," Benny said.

Melody nodded and smiled. "Then it's settled." She looked around. "I wonder what's keeping Victor," she said.

"Who's Victor?" Soo Lee asked.

"Victor Perrelli, the conductor," Violet told her.

"Was he at the hotel?" Mr. Alden asked.

"He took a later plane," Melody said. "But he should be here by now."

Just then, a large man entered. His gray hair stood up at odd angles. He wore a rumpled sweater and slacks, and a pair of old sneakers. He stood just inside the door looking uncertain. And he was humming!

"Oh, there he is," Melody said, and headed toward hm.

Mr. Alden, who was on the welcoming committee, followed her.

"That's the great Victor Perrelli?" Henry said aloud.

They were all surprised. This man was *not* what they had expected.

"I wonder why he's dressed like that," Violet said.

Everyone else was dressed up.

"Maybe he didn't know about the party," Jessie suggested.

"Let's find out," Benny said.

They went over to join the others.

"Oh, Victor, I was wondering where you were," Melody was saying. "Did you forget about the party?"

"Oh," he answered mumbling. "I started

thinking about the Mozart symphony. We need to work on the tempo before the concert."

"We have plenty of time for that," Melody assured him. "The concert is Friday evening — that's five days away."

"I'm afraid I got so involved that I lost track of time," Victor explained. "Then, I couldn't find my luggage anywhere."

"Did you remember to pick it up at the airport?" Melody asked.

Mr. Perrelli ran his hands through his hair. "Did I? Now, let me think."

"No, you didn't remember," a voice said, "but I did." A man carrying a suitcase and a garment bag came up beside them.

Victor said, "Thank you," and wandered off toward the food table, humming.

Melody sighed. "What would he do without you, Bob?" she said.

Looking at them over his half glasses, the man shrugged.

"This is Bob Weldon," Melody said to the Aldens.

Bob Weldon said, "Hello." Then he hurried off, saying, "I have to check the auditorium."

"Is he a musician?" Violet asked.

"No," Melody answered. "He's our manager."

"What does a manager do?" Soo Lee asked.

"Everything!" Melody answered. "He schedules our tours. Makes sure we get where we're going and that everything is right when we get there. Sometimes, he settles arguments. The orchestra couldn't do without him."

"It sounds like an interesting job," Henry said.

"It sounds like a hard job," Benny put in.

Melody laughed. "It's both those things."

"Mr. Weldon doesn't seem to like it very much," Soo Lee said.

"He *is* a little grumpy at times," Melody said. "I don't think he knows how much we appreciate him."

"We certainly couldn't have scheduled this week without him," Mr. Alden said. "He helped us plan everything."

"I'll show you something else he helped plan," Melody said as she started across the room. "It's what makes this tour *extra* special."

The Aldens were puzzled. It seemed to them that everything about this tour was extra special.

CHAPTER 3

The Score

Melody led them to the lobby. She stopped before a glass case on the wall.

Pointing to several sheets of music displayed inside, she said, "Look at those!"

"Aren't they amazing?" a woman who had been staring at them said.

Benny didn't see anything special about the papers. He opened his mouth to say so but decided not to.

Violet moved closer for a better look. "They *are* wonderful," she said.

The woman turned to face them. When

she saw Melody, her face reddened. "Oh, dear," she said. "I — uh — You're Ms. Carmody!"

Melody smiled. "Yes," she said. "How did you know?"

"I've — uh — seen your picture," she explained. She sounded very nervous. "I'm Janet Muller," she went on. "I own an antique store in town."

Melody smiled. "Well, this Mozart score is certainly an antique," she said.

Benny knew about keeping score in baseball, but he didn't think that had anything to do with music. "What does she mean, 'this Mozart score'?" he asked Violet.

"It's a written piece of music, which musicians play from," his sister explained.

"And this one even has Mozart's signature on it," Janet Muller said. "See, right here. Isn't it beautiful?"

"Yes," Jessie marveled. "It really is."

What was so exciting about a man's name on a piece of paper, Benny wondered. He stood on tiptoe for a better look. "I can't even read his name," he said.

Violet pointed out the letters of the composer's last name. "It says *Mozart*," she told him.

"Mozart, Mozart," Benny sang. "Doesn't he have more than *one* name?"

"Indeed, he does," Victor Perrelli's voice boomed. "His whole name is Joannes Chrysostomus Wolfgang Gottlieb Mozart."

Benny's eyes grew wide. "That's some name!" he said.

Victor laughed. "It's a good thing I don't have a name like that. I'd never remember it," he said. Then he wandered off again, humming.

"No one ever called him by his full name," Janet Muller put in. "He was known as Wolfgang Amadeus Mozart."

"Where'd they get the Amadeus part?" Benny asked.

"Amadeus is the Latin form of Gottlieb," Melody explained. "I guess his family decided they liked it better."

"How did you get hold of the score?" Janet asked.

"We have Bob Weldon to thank for that,"

Melody answered. "We play a lot of Mozart's music. Bob talked a museum into loaning us this original score to take on tour."

"This whole thing is so exciting," Janet Muller said. She leaned close as though she were about to share a secret. "I collect autographs." She opened the book she was holding. On each page was a signature. "Here's the famous Victor Perrelli's," she said proudly. She thrust the book toward Melody. "May I have *your* autograph?"

Melody stepped back. "You don't want my signature," she said. "I'm nobody famous."

"Someday maybe," Janet said. "You just never know. I'll bet Mozart never realized something he wrote would be so valuable."

Melody took the book and the pen Janet held out to her. "Well, if you put it that way," she said, and signed her name.

Janet Muller looked at the signature. She traced Melody's name with a forefinger. "Thank you," she said.

"Thank *you*," Melody responded. "You are the very first person who has ever asked for my autograph."

Once again, Janet studied the Mozart score. "Aren't you afraid someone will steal it?" she asked. "I mean . . . is there security or anything? Someone watching it?"

Melody said only, "It's safe."

"Oh, look!" Janet said. "There's Abner Medina!" She raced off, her autograph book open to a blank page.

"Who's Abner Medina?" Benny asked.

"The best percussionist in the country," Melody answered.

"Percussion? Like drums and things?" Jessie asked.

Melody nodded.

Benny moved his hands as though he were beating a drum. "I'd like to do that," he said.

Henry laughed. "You make enough noise as it is," he teased.

"It's only noise when you're not good," Melody said. "I think Benny would be good."

Benny made a *so-there* face at Henry.

Everyone laughed.

Melody looked at her watch. "Oh, dear," she said. "I'm as bad as Victor. I get involved and forget what I'm supposed to do. I have to go. If I don't practice, I'll never be able to play my solo." She told them all good-bye, and, promising to see them soon, she hurried away.

The Aldens turned their attention back to the Mozart score.

"What did that lady mean when she said this was valuable?" Soo Lee asked.

"The score is worth a lot of money," Henry said.

"What makes it worth so much?" Benny asked. "It's just a bunch of papers with musical notes on them."

"It's very old," Henry said. "Mozart was born in 1756, over two hundred years ago."

"Wow!" Benny exclaimed.

"Mozart is one of the greatest composers ever," Jessie added. "And this music isn't a copy; it's in his own handwriting."

"You won't believe how young he was when he started writing music," Violet said.

"How old?" Benny asked.

"Five years old," Violet told him. "He was

probably composing music in his head before that."

Amazed, Soo Lee and Benny looked at one another. Mozart was younger than either of them when he began writing music!

Benny leaned in for a better look at the score. "He didn't write this one when he was five," he said. "It's too neat. There's nothing crossed out or erased."

"Mozart didn't make mistakes," Violet said. "The music just flowed out of his mind onto the paper."

Benny shook his head. "I could never do that," he said. "Even in my mind, I make mistakes!"

CHAPTER 4

The Missing Score

Later, at home, the Alden children sat around the kitchen table drinking hot chocolate. Soo Lee, who was staying overnight, was with them.

"That was a great party," Jessie said.

"The food was super," Benny said. "Too bad there's none left. The jelly sandwiches were the best."

"I liked meeting the musicians," Violet put in. "Especially Melody."

"She's nice," Soo Lee said. "I can't wait to hear her play her violin."

24

"You won't have a long wait, Soo Lee," Henry said. "Tomorrow morning, we'll go to the orchestra's rehearsal."

"You know what I don't get," Benny said. "Melody said she had to go practice."

"All musicians practice, Benny," Jessie said. "You know that."

"But what's rehearsal?" Benny asked.

"Practice," Henry answered.

"So musicians practice for the practice," Benny said.

Henry laughed. "It looks that way," he said.

Violet disagreed. "Musicians practice for themselves," she said. "To get better."

"It works, too," Jessie said. "Violet's a perfect example."

"I wish I could play as well as Violet," Soo Lee said.

"You will," Jessie assured her. "It takes time."

"And practice," Benny added. He poured himself more hot chocolate. "I have another question," he said. "How does Victor Perrelli practice?"

They were all silent, thinking.

Finally, Violet said, "A conductor listens to music and thinks about it. That's a way of practicing."

"What about Mozart?" Soo Lee asked. "How did he practice?"

"His father was a music teacher," Violet told her. "He learned to play early."

"But writing music isn't the same as playing it," Benny said.

"It's like a language," Henry explained. "You hear it first. Then you learn to speak it. Finally, you learn to write it. And the more you write it, the better you get."

Soo Lee understood that. Her first language was Korean. She had learned to speak English at the orphanage. Only now was she learning to write it well. She sighed. "Everything takes practice," she said.

Watch sidled over and put his paw in Jessie's lap. He looked up at her and softly whined.

"It must be suppertime," Jessie said, and looked at the clock. Sure enough, it was nearly six. "I'll go boil some water for spaghetti."

Mrs. McGregor, the Aldens' housekeeper, was on vacation, so the children were doing their own cooking.

Henry groaned. "Who can eat after all that party food?" he said.

Benny popped to his feet. "I can!" he answered.

"Now I know why Benny's such a good eater," Violet said. "He gets so much practice."

Next morning, Benny and Soo Lee were the first ones out the door. They were anxious to get to the Civic Center to hear the orchestra rehearse. Now that they knew some of the musicians, it would be a special treat to see and hear them play.

At the corner, Benny saw the bus coming. He waved to the others, urging them to hurry.

They picked up their pace, arriving just

as the bus pulled in and stopped. The five Aldens piled on.

"The workshops begin after the rehearsal," Jessie reminded them, when they had taken their seats.

"I'm taking Make Your Own Instruments," Benny said.

"I'd like to take Music Appreciation," Soo Lee said.

"I'm going to all the rehearsals," Jessie said.

"We can go to all the workshops and still hear the rehearsals," Henry told them. "Each one is at a different time."

Violet was silent, thinking about the week ahead. On Saturday afternoon, there would be a special children's performance. She hoped to be chosen as a violinist, but she was afraid to mention it. It seemed like an impossible dream. Still, it might come true. She had wished that one of the musicians would ask to hear her play. That had come true. She wondered when she'd have a chance to play for Melody.

"Civic Center," the bus driver announced.

Saying, "Thank you," the Aldens hopped off the bus. They raced each other to the Center's big front doors.

The lobby was full of people. Everyone seemed to be in a panic. Orchestra members stood around in small groups talking excitedly. Victor Perrelli paced the floor murmuring to himself. Melody followed a few steps behind. They couldn't hear what she was saying to Victor, but they could tell she was upset.

Janet Muller stood near them. "I was afraid of something like this," she said.

"What is it?" Jessie asked. "What's happened?"

"The Mozart score," she answered. "It's been stolen!"

CHAPTER 5

The Search

"The Mozart score has been stolen?" Jessie repeated to make sure she had heard right.

"Yes," Janet Muller said. She wandered away, murmuring, "I knew it. I just knew this would happen."

Melody saw the Aldens and rushed over.

"When did you discover the score was stolen?" Jessie asked.

"Do you know who stole it?" Benny added.

"Have you called the police?" Henry wanted to know.

Melody held up her hand to silence them. "Wait, wait," she said. "Who told you the score had been stolen?"

"Janet Muller," Jessie answered.

"She's jumping to conclusions," Melody said.

"The score *hasn't* been stolen then!" Violet sounded relieved.

Henry looked at the display case. It was empty. "The score's not in the case," he said. "If it wasn't stolen, where is it?"

Melody shrugged. "We're not sure," she said. Then she went on to explain. "Victor took it back to the hotel after the party. He thought it would be safer than leaving it here at the Center overnight."

Bob Weldon came up beside Melody. "Too bad no one was around to remind the *great* Victor Perrelli not to misplace it," he said.

Benny nodded. "He forgot where he put it!"

"It shouldn't be too difficult to find," Henry said.

Melody sighed. "Victor's the only one who knows where it is, and he has completely forgotten."

"Maybe he'll remember where he put it when he starts looking for it," Jessie suggested.

Bob Weldon chuckled. "By the time he gets back to the hotel, he'll forget why he's there," he said.

"We could go back to the hotel with Mr. Perrelli," Henry suggested.

"Yes," Violet said. "We could help him look."

Benny thought that was a splendid idea. "We'll find the missing music," he assured Melody. "We're very good detectives."

Melody smiled. "I'll get Victor," she said.

"What about the rehearsal?" Bob Weldon asked. "We can't cancel that. People are arriving. We can't disappoint them."

Melody's smile faded. "You're right, Bob. If we cancel the first event of the week . . ." Her voice trailed off.

"So the score will have to wait," Bob Weldon said. "I'll round up the musicians." He hurried off.

"I hate to put off looking for the score," Melody said. "The longer it's lost, the greater the chance that the wrong person might find it."

"Couldn't someone else conduct the rehearsal?" Violet asked.

"That's it," Melody said. "I've been so upset, I don't seem to be thinking. I'll lead the rehearsal while you and Victor go back to the hotel." She hurried over to Victor to tell him the plan.

He listened attentively, and nodded. Then he strode toward the Aldens. "Let's see what we can see," he said and led them outside.

At the hotel, they went directly to his room. There, the conductor turned the doorknob and pushed open the door.

Henry was surprised. "The door wasn't locked," he said.

Victor Perrelli stepped back to let the children enter. "Locked doors require keys," he said. "Too easy to misplace."

"But anyone could come into your room, Mr. Perrelli," Jessie said. "Maybe — "

"Please call me Victor," he interrupted. He walked into the room. "What we need here is music!" He snapped on the tape recorder on the nightstand.

Instantly, the room was filled with the sounds of a full orchestra. Victor stood listening, his eyes closed. After several seconds, he began to wave his arms as though he were conducting the invisible musicians.

The children waited silently. Finally, Benny whispered, "Now I know how he practices."

Victor dropped his arms suddenly and turned to the Aldens. "What was it we were supposed to do here?"

"Look for the missing score," Henry reminded him.

Victor nodded. "Oh, yes, of course. Where shall we look first?"

"Try to remember what you did when you came back here after the reception," Jessie suggested.

Victor nodded. "I listened to a Mozart concerto," he said. "Very beautiful."

"Did you hide the score before or after that?" Violet asked.

Victor sighed deeply. "A head full of music has no room for details," he answered.

Seeing that they could not depend on Victor to remember anything helpful, Henry took charge. "Let's divide things up," he suggested. "Jessie and Soo Lee, you check the bathroom. Violet, you help Victor search this room. Benny and I will look in the closet."

They all set to work.

Jessie and Soo Lee found nothing in the bathroom.

Violet and Victor looked everywhere — even under the mattress. No success.

Henry and Benny searched the closet shelves and Mr. Perrelli's pockets. Nothing. Finally, Benny dragged the suitcase into the room.

"How about in here?" he asked.

Victor opened the suitcase. It was empty.

"Your garment bag's hanging in the closet," Henry said. "We didn't look in it."

Victor shook his head. "There's nothing in there but my tuxedo. And it's dirty at that. I must remember to have it cleaned before the concert." Suddenly, his face lit up. "Yes, yes. Now I remember."

He had remembered where he'd put the score! The Aldens waited anxiously for him to tell them where it was.

Instead, he said, "Such a strange thing: memory."

"What is it you remembered?" Henry asked.

"Last night, after I listened to the concerto, I took a long walk," Victor responded. "It was a lovely night. It brought back so many memories of my childhood."

"Did you lock your door when you left?" Jessie asked.

She knew the answer. They all knew the answer. Victor Perrelli did not lock his door.

Had someone come into his room while he was out and found the Mozart score? Perhaps Janet Muller had been right after all: The music *had* been stolen!

CHAPTER 6

Two Suspects

Victor Perrelli sank to the edge of the bed. "Oh, my," he said, and ran his hands through his hair. "Do you suppose someone came in here and took the score?"

"We've looked everywhere," Jessie said. "It doesn't seem to be here."

"This is terrible, terrible," Victor said. "But who would do such a thing?"

"The score is very valuable," Henry said. "Many people might like to have it."

Victor popped to his feet. "Great music belongs to the world," he said. "This cannot be! I will *not* let this happen!" He strode out of the room.

The Aldens followed at his heels, out of the hotel.

As they marched back to the Civic Center, Benny said, "Don't worry. We'll help you find the music."

But now the great Victor Perrelli was humming, and he didn't seem to hear.

Back at the Civic Center, Melody was talking on the lobby phone. When she saw them, she looked nervous, and abruptly stopped talking. As they came closer she hung up quickly and hurried over. It seemed as though she had been caught doing something she shouldn't.

"Oh, there you are," she said. "I was just — "

"Why is there no music?" Victor demanded. "We must rehearse!"

Melody's face was nearly as red as her hair. "We took a break," she explained. "Now that you're here, Victor, you can take over." Her voice was sharp.

Without another word, Victor headed into the auditorium.

Melody started after him.

"Don't you want to hear what happened?" Benny asked her.

Melody halted. "Yes, of course," she said. "Did you find the score?"

"We looked everywhere," Jessie answered. "But we couldn't find it."

"Victor doesn't lock his door," Henry told her. "Anyone could have walked off with it."

"I can't worry about that now," Melody said. "I have to rehearse!" She stomped off.

"She's acting a bit strange," Henry said.

"She's probably worried about the missing music," Violet defended.

"She can't be too worried," Benny said. "She didn't even ask us about it."

"You can't think *she* took it," Violet said. "Why would she do that?"

No one had an answer.

"What about the phone call?" Jessie asked. "It looked as though we'd caught her in the middle of something she wanted to keep secret."

"Melody was probably just calling the hotel looking for us," Violet suggested.

Soo Lee nodded. "That would mean she *is* worried about the score."

"Of course she is," Violet said. "That's why she phoned: She wanted to know if we'd found it."

"Funny she didn't say something when we got back here," Jessie said.

"Victor didn't give her much of a chance to say anything," Henry reminded her.

Music drifted into the lobby.

"Let's talk about this later," Jessie suggested. "I want to hear the rehearsal."

The Aldens went into the auditorium.

Victor was at the podium. "Let's try it once more," he was saying. He took up his baton. "Now, remember, this passage should be sweet, full of heart." He waited until everyone was ready. Then, with a downward stroke of the baton, he started the music again.

The Aldens sat quietly. Music surrounded them. They felt as though they were being lifted up and carried away to beautiful new places.

Victor tapped his baton against the podium. "No, no!" he said. "The strings are coming in late. Ms. Carmody, are you with us?"

Melody mumbled an apology.

"It sounded good to me," Benny said.

"But Victor has a trained ear," Violet said. "He hears things we don't."

"I don't know how he can conduct at all with the missing score on his mind," Jessie put in.

"He's probably forgotten all about it," Henry said.

Jessie wasn't so sure. "He seemed awfully upset about it at the hotel. How could he forget it so soon?"

"He remembers all that music," Soo Lee said.

"And Mozart's long name," Benny added. "But nothing else."

"Do you suppose . . . ?" Violet said.

"No," Henry answered firmly. "Victor

didn't steal the score. We shouldn't even think it."

"Nobody would think it," Jessie said. "Maybe he knows that."

"Right," Benny piped up. "Maybe he just pretends to be so forgetful to throw everyone off the trail."

"I think he really is forgetful," Henry argued. "Remember what he said: 'A head full of music has no room for details.' "

"Is valuable missing music just a detail?" Soo Lee wanted to know.

No one, not even Victor Perrelli, could answer yes to that.

They fell silent as the music began again. But their heads buzzed with unanswered questions.

CHAPTER 7

Violet's Lesson

At lunchtime, the orchestra stopped practicing. Most of the members went back to the hotel. Bob Weldon suggested that he and Victor make one last search for the score. The Aldens looked for Melody to ask her to have lunch with them, but she had disappeared.

They walked to a nearby coffee shop.

After they had placed their orders, Violet said, "Melody looked upset when Victor corrected her."

"You mean about the violins coming in late?" Henry asked.

Violet nodded. "Maybe that's why she disappeared like she did after the rehearsal."

"But Victor corrected everyone," Soo Lee piped up.

"Right," Benny agreed. "If they all got upset about it, the whole orchestra would have disappeared."

"Benny's right. Something else is bothering Melody," Jessie said. "If only we could figure out what it is."

Just then, the waiter brought their lunches, big sandwiches with potato chips on the side. Although Benny's sandwich was larger than the others, he was the first one finished.

"Let's go," he said as he wiped his chin.

"We have plenty of time," Henry told him. "The workshop won't start for half an hour."

"But it might be filled up if we don't get there early," Benny said.

He had a point. The auditorium had been nearly full during rehearsal.

The Aldens finished their lunches and hurried back to the Civic Center.

Abner Medina, the percussionist they'd seen the day before, was in charge of the Make Your Own Instruments workshop. "I'm very happy to see so many eager faces," he said.

He went on to demonstrate some homemade instruments. He showed them a harmonica made from a comb and wax paper; a cigar box guitar; paper plate tambourines; and drinking glass chimes.

"You can even make music with a rubber band," he said and looped a rubber band over two fingers. He spread them wide and strummed the rubber band with the fingers of his other hand.

"How about drums?" Benny asked. "I want to make drums."

Abner Medina looked pleased. "Everything you need is on this table," he said. "Get to work. Use your imaginations. See what you can come up with."

Violet was selecting her materials when Melody came into the room. Smiling

warmly, she no longer seemed upset.

"Violet," she said, "why don't you come back to the hotel with me now? I'd like to hear you play."

Violet was thrilled by the invitation. At the same time, she was nervous about it. What if she froze and couldn't play? What if Melody didn't think she played well?

"Oh, I'd love to," she said, "but I didn't bring my violin."

"I'm sure I can find one for you," Melody told her. "I'll go see what I can do and meet you in the lobby. How's that sound?"

It sounded wonderful. "All right," Violet said.

Melody turned to the Aldens' new cousin. "Would you like to come along, Soo Lee?" she asked.

"Oh, yes," Soo Lee answered.

Saying, "Give me five minutes," Melody left the room.

"She's being awfully nice," Jessie commented.

"She *is* nice," Violet said.

"But this morning when we came back

from the hotel, she hardly said a word to us," Henry reminded his sister.

"She was upset about Victor," Violet said. "We already decided that."

"Maybe we were wrong," Benny said. "Maybe she did take the music, and she's being nice now because she's afraid we suspect her."

"That isn't true!" Violet cried. Taking Soo Lee's hand, she hurried out to the lobby.

Except for the decorating, Melody's hotel room was much like Victor's. Violet and Soo Lee liked this room better. It was done in shades of purple.

"Try this for size," Melody said as she handed Violet a violin.

Violet secured the instrument between her left shoulder and her chin. "It seems fine," she said.

"It looks fine, too." Melody handed Violet a bow. "Now let's hear how it sounds." She sat down beside Soo Lee on the small couch.

Violet ran the bow across the strings. The

violin squeaked. She lifted the bow. "I'm sorry," she said. "That's an awful sound."

"I make sounds like that all the time," Soo Lee said.

Melody laughed. "Don't feel bad," she said. "Even the best violinists manage a squeak now and then."

Violet tried again. This time the sound was not noise but music. At the end of the piece, Melody came to stand beside her. She adjusted Violet's hand on the bow.

"Relax your wrist, Violet," she instructed. "There. That's much better. Now play another — "

The telephone rang. Melody picked it up. "Hello." After a few seconds, she said, "Oh — uh — yes, I'm glad you called, but" — She turned her back on the girls and lowered her voice — "I — uh — can't talk now . . . As I said this morning, we should meet . . . About what we discussed, yes . . ."

Violet felt uncomfortable. She knew she and Soo Lee shouldn't be hearing this conversation, but they couldn't help it. She motioned her cousin over to the far window, where they stood looking out on Greenfield's Main Street.

"The sooner the better," Melody was saying. "The whole thing makes me nervous. . . . But what if someone finds out?"

A wave of doubt washed over Violet. Could her sister and brothers be right? Was Melody the thief?

Lowering her voice until it was almost a whisper, Melody said, "Yes, all right. The town square. Eight-thirty tomorrow morning. . . . Oh, don't worry, I'll be there."

Melody hung up and turned around. She took a deep breath. "All right," she said, smiling uneasily. "Let's get back to our lesson."

CHAPTER 8

Spies

An hour later, when Violet and Soo Lee returned to the Civic Center, the other Aldens were outside waiting for them.

"Finally!" Benny said as his sister and cousin approached.

"That must have been some lesson," Henry added.

"That's for sure," Violet responded. "And you'll never guess what happened." She told them about the mysterious phone call and Melody's reaction to it.

They were all shocked. It was one thing

to imagine someone might be guilty; it was another to have proof. And this new information did, indeed, seem like proof.

No one said a word until they were on the bus headed home.

Then, Jessie asked Violet, "Did Melody say she and the caller talked this morning?"

Violet remembered the exact words. " 'As I said this morning, we should meet.' "

Soo Lee nodded. "That is what Melody said."

"That telephone call this morning from the Civic Center lobby . . ." Henry did not finish his thought.

It wasn't necessary. They were all thinking the same thing: Melody had not been phoning the hotel looking for them; she had been talking to that afternoon's mysterious caller.

"We should tell Grandfather," Benny said.

"What if we're wrong?" Violet asked. She did not want to believe that Melody was the thief. "Soo Lee and I heard only one side of the conversation."

Jessie drew in a long breath. "It's hard to know what to do."

They fell silent, thinking. By the time they reached their stop, Henry had an idea.

"We should check this out before we tell anyone," he said.

Everyone agreed.

"Where did you say Melody was meeting the caller?" he asked Violet.

"The town square at eight-thirty tomorrow morning."

Henry nodded. "All right, then. We'll be there at eight-fifteen."

"Henry," Jessie said, "what if they see us?"

"They won't see us," Benny assured her. "There're plenty of places to hide."

At home, Grandfather Alden was reading the newspaper. Watch sat by the door.

"I knew you'd be along soon," Mr. Alden said when the young Aldens came into the kitchen. "Watch was napping until ten minutes ago. Then he woke up and went to wait by the door."

Watch wagged his tail.

Benny patted him. "Good boy," he said.

"Mozart's dog did that," Violet said. "I read in a book that he always seemed to know when Mozart was on his way home."

"How was the rehearsal?" Mr. Alden asked.

"We didn't get to hear much of it," Jessie answered.

Henry told him about the missing music and their search for it. He did not mention Melody's mysterious phone call.

Mr. Alden shook his head slowly. "How unfortunate!" he said. "The loss of that score is bound to upset everyone."

"That's for sure," Benny said. "I'm so upset, I'm hungry, and it's not even suppertime."

"I can understand that," said Mr. Alden. "All that thinking would make anyone hungry." He sounded serious, but there was a teasing twinkle in his eye.

"If you can wait an hour, Benny, I'll make my specialty," Henry said.

Benny grinned. "Chicken and Swiss

cheese with all that good sauce on top?"

Watch barked.

Benny laughed. "Even Watch knows that's worth waiting for."

"Violet, why don't you go practice?" Jessie suggested. "We'll handle things down here."

"I'll set the table," Soo Lee offered.

"Thanks," Violet said. "I can use all the practice I can get if I'm going to make the young people's orchestra."

She hurried up to her room. In a few minutes, the sweet sounds of her violin drifted into the kitchen.

During dinner, Benny told Grandfather Alden about the instrument-making class. "I made a drum from an empty coffee can," he said. "It sounds good, too."

Mr. Alden was pleased. "I've always said my grandchildren know how to make something from nothing," he said proudly. "That's a good trait for getting along in life."

"We learned how to do that when we lived in the boxcar," Violet said.

Mr. Alden nodded. "I hate to think of you children living like that — all alone," he said.

"But you did learn useful lessons there."

"And we found you," Benny reminded him.

Mr. Alden reached over and put an arm around his youngest grandchild. "I'm certainly glad of that."

"I'm glad, too," Soo Lee put in.

"So are we!" the others all said.

The next morning, the children caught the first bus to the town square. During the ride, they decided to hide in the town hall, which opened early.

No one was around when they entered the building. Quietly, they took up positions near the double front doors. From the windows beside them, they could see all but a small corner of the square.

After a few minutes, Benny whispered, "Look!"

A man in a dark hat and raincoat entered the square. Under his arm, he carried a large envelope.

"What do you suppose he has in that envelope?" Henry wondered aloud.

"I'll bet it's money," Benny said.

The man looked around, glanced at his watch, and began to pace.

"Maybe Melody won't come," Violet said. There was a hopeful note in her voice.

Just then, Melody came into view. She hurried over to meet the man. They shook hands and spoke briefly.

"Too bad we can't hear what they're saying," Jessie said.

"We don't need to," Henry responded. "Look!"

Melody took an envelope out of her bag and gave it to the man. In return, he gave her his envelope.

"I'll bet she's selling him the score!" Benny said.

CHAPTER 9

The Invitation

"Now, we *have* to tell Grandfather about Melody and the mysterious man," Jessie said as they walked to the Civic Center.

Benny had another idea. "We should call the police! That's what we should do!"

"We can't do that," Violet protested. "We don't know what was in those envelopes."

"You're right, Violet," agreed Jessie. "We can't accuse Melody without proof."

"Maybe we should talk to her," Henry said. "Tell her what we saw. If she didn't steal the score, she'll explain what's going on."

"And if she did steal it?" Soo Lee wanted to know.

"Then we're in hot water," Henry said.

Soo Lee looked puzzled. "Hot water?" she repeated.

They were at the Civic Center.

"I'll explain later," Henry told her as they went inside.

The musicians were assembled on the stage. Melody was in her proper place to Victor's left. The Aldens thought she had a guilty look on her face.

Janet Muller slid into the aisle beside Jessie. "I don't suppose there's anything new on the missing score?"

"Nothing," Jessie answered.

Then, Victor hit a downbeat and the music began. This rehearsal went well. After it was over, the audience clapped loudly.

Victor stepped to the edge of the stage. "I can see you are easily pleased," he said, but it was obvious that he, too, was happy. He turned to the orchestra. "Take a long lunch," he told them. It was his way of saying they had played well.

Today, lunch was set up in the reception hall. Benny walked beside the long table looking at the food. There were salads of all kinds: vegetable, pasta, egg, tuna, bean, and potato. At either end was a large meat and cheese tray. Baskets held different kinds of bread. Fruit filled several bowls.

Jessie filled her plate with pasta salad and rye bread. "What're you going to have, Benny?" Jessie asked.

Benny shook his head. "It all looks so good, I can't decide."

"Which means you've decided to have some of everything," Henry said.

Benny pretended he hadn't thought of that. "What a good idea, Henry," he said and began to take samples of every single dish.

They took their plates to chairs along the wall.

Just then, Melody came in from the auditorium with Janet Muller. They headed toward the Aldens.

"There you are!" Melody said as though she'd been looking for them. "How would you like to meet me at the hotel early tomorrow? They set out rolls and juice every morning. We could eat and then come back here. I'm going to try my solo on stage. I could use an audience."

"We'd love to!" Violet exclaimed. She was sure Melody couldn't be the thief.

CHAPTER 10

Mixed Messages

That afternoon, the children attended the Music Appreciation workshop in the auditorium. As they slid into their seats, Victor tapped his baton for attention. The audience fell silent. "In order to appreciate music," he began, "one should know something about the orchestra playing it."

First he introduced the different sections. There were the strings — violins and cellos — and the woodwinds — flutes, clarinets, and oboes. There was also the brass, which included French horns and trumpets, and

Benny's favorite, the percussion, with instruments such as drums and the triangle. Each section played a musical passage. Then, Victor talked about the different kinds of music.

The Aldens became so interested they forgot about the missing score until they returned home. After a supper of hot dogs and beans, they settled by the fire.

Curled up in a big chair, Soo Lee said, "What does it mean to be in hot water?" She was remembering their earlier conversation.

Benny, who was sprawled on the floor, put his chin in his hands. "Well, Soo Lee, it's like this," he said. After a pause, he turned to his brother. "You explain it, Henry."

Henry laughed. "Being in hot water is the same as being in trouble."

Jessie added, "We saw Melody exchange envelopes with that strange man. If she took the music and was selling it or something, she would be angry that we knew."

Soo Lee nodded. "And we'd be in hot water!"

"You got it," Benny said.

They grew silent. The fire crackled. Shadows danced across the walls and ceiling. After awhile, Henry suggested they go over the clues.

They recounted all they knew. Nothing fit together. Victor had taken the score back to the hotel. Yet, it seemed unlikely that he now knew where it was. Melody had met the mysterious man and given him something. Still, they couldn't imagine why she would have taken the music.

"So let's say neither Melody nor Victor is the thief," Jessie summed up. "Then who is?"

Benny sighed heavily. "This is a hard one," he said. "We'll never solve it."

"We're good detectives, Benny," Henry reminded him. "We'll solve it."

Benny yawned. "Not tonight we won't." He yawned again, put his head on his arms, and fell asleep.

Henry carried him upstairs to his room. The others followed. They were all too tired, they decided, to think another thought.

* * *

In the morning, once again, they took the bus to the hotel.

Benny was impatient to get there. "I'm hungry," he said.

"There will be rolls and juice in the lobby," Violet reminded him.

But Benny didn't need reminding. "That's what made me hungry," he said. "I was thinking about it."

"Me, too," Soo Lee agreed.

They entered the hotel just as Janet Muller was leaving.

"Ms. Muller!" Jessie was unable to hide her surprise. "What are you doing here so early?"

Janet Muller's face turned red. "Oh — I — uh . . ." she stammered.

"Bet you came for the sweet rolls," Benny said.

She cleared her throat nervously. "Autographs," she explained. "I came for autographs."

Henry glanced around the empty lobby. "Were you able to get any?" he asked.

Janet shook her head. "I think I'll go over

to the Civic Center. Maybe someone will show up there."

"See you later," Benny said, and skipped over to the breakfast buffet.

Soo Lee followed at his heels.

Janet Muller didn't move. She stood there as though she were about to say something.

Finally, Henry asked, "Is there something we can do for you?"

"Oh, no, thank you," Janet said. "I was just — uh — wondering." She cleared her throat again. "About the score — have they found out anything?"

The Aldens all shook their heads.

Janet asked several more questions. No one had the answers. When Melody stepped off the elevator, Janet mumbled something and sailed out the door.

"That was strange," Henry commented.

"She seemed awfully nervous," Violet added.

"You don't suppose . . . ?" Violet asked.

Jessie finished her sister's incomplete question. "That Janet Muller is the thief? I don't know."

They joined Melody, Soo Lee, and Benny at the table. The Aldens ate heartily.

Melody didn't take a single bite. She was too nervous about her solo, she explained. "And I wanted to talk to Victor, but I can't find him," she added.

"Maybe he's at the Center," Henry suggested.

"He told me he was going to have breakfast in his room."

"Maybe he forgot," Soo Lee suggested.

Melody laughed. "You're probably right, Soo Lee."

"Do you want to wait for him?" Jessie asked.

"No," Melody replied. "Let's go. I have to practice."

Victor was pacing up and down in front of the Civic Center. "There you are, Melody!" he said as they approached.

"Victor! What are you doing here?" Melody asked.

Victor looked confused. "You asked me to meet you here."

"Yes, this *afternoon*."

"He really is forgetful," Benny whispered to Henry. "It's not an act, that's for sure."

"No, no!" Victor fished in his coat pocket. "You sent me this message." He pulled out a notepaper and handed it to Melody. "Someone from the hotel slipped it under my door."

"Victor, meet me at the Civic Center, 8:00 A.M. *Urgent!"* Melody read aloud. "It's dated today. And that looks like my signature, all right. But I did not write this note!"

CHAPTER 11

False Notes

Victor ran his fingers through his hair. "You did not write this note," he repeated.

"No, I most certainly did not," Melody answered. "Why would I?"

"I thought perhaps you wanted to meet to talk to me about the orchestra," Victor said. "About how . . . unhappy you are."

Melody looked surprised. "Unhappy? What makes you think I'm . . . unhappy, Victor?"

"My dear, you have been with the or-

chestra a long time. I know you well." Victor
put his arm around Melody's shoulders.
"Now, let's get on with your practice." He
led her off toward the theater.

"What was all that about?" Benny wanted
to know.

"Someone wrote Victor a note and signed
Melody's name," Jessie answered.

Benny shook his head. That was not what
he had meant. "About Melody being unhappy. She doesn't look unhappy."

"We can talk about that later," Henry said.
"Now, we have to figure out who wrote that
note."

"And why," Jessie added.

Violin music drifted into the room.

Violet said, "Oh, we're missing Melody's
practice," and hurried toward the auditorium.

The others followed. Perhaps an idea
would come to them as they listened to Melody's solo performance.

They slipped into front row seats. Down
the aisle, Victor's head was bowed, and his

eyes were closed. They thought he might be sleeping. On stage, Melody swayed gently as she played. She moved the bow over the strings with a light, sure touch. Under her skillful fingers, the violin seemed to come alive.

"I'll never be able to play like that," Violet whispered.

"Sure you will," Henry said. "It just takes practice."

Suddenly, Benny blurted, "I know!"

Jessie, who was sitting beside him, said, "Benny, hush!"

"But I know why — !"

Violet leaned around her sister. "Shhh!" she commanded.

Grumbling to himself, Benny slumped back in his seat.

After awhile, Melody lifted her bow from the violin. Victor was on his feet before the last notes had died away.

"My dear, that was superb!" he said. "There's just one passage that still needs work." He climbed the stage stairs to show

Melody which part of the music he wanted her to try again.

Benny looked at the other Aldens. "Can I talk now?"

"What do you want to tell us?" Henry asked.

"I know why someone sent that note to Victor: To get him out of his room!"

"That makes sense," Jessie said, "but why would anyone want Victor to leave his room?"

"Whoever did it might think the missing score is still there," Violet suggested.

Benny nodded vigorously. "And they wanted to search for it!"

They decided to tell Victor and Melody what they suspected.

Victor listened intently. Then he nodded and said, "We must go back to the hotel immediately!" and ran up the aisle.

Melody and the Aldens ran after him.

But they were too late. Back at the hotel, they found Victor's door standing open. Inside, the room was a jumble. Drawers were overturned, their contents strewn about the floor. Sheets and pillows were pulled off the bed. Clothes lay in piles on the closet floor.

Victor picked up his garment bag and unzipped it. His tuxedo was in a heap at the bottom.

Bob Weldon came into the room. Looking at the mess over his glasses, he said, "Not you, too!"

"You mean your room was ransacked?" Melody asked.

"Yes," Bob answered. "I went down to the dining room to meet you as you asked, Melody, and — "

"I never asked you to meet me," Melody interrupted.

Bob looked confused. "But your note — it said you had to see me immediately."

"I didn't write you a note," Melody told him.

Still confused, Bob said, "I don't have time to argue. There is too much to do." He started to leave.

"Wait!" Victor called. "This tuxedo needs cleaning before the dress rehearsal. Please see to it." He handed Bob the garment bag.

Bob narrowed his eyes. "Yes, sir," he said. Under his breath, he added, "Always waits till the last minute," just loud enough for the Aldens to hear.

"We had better get back to the Civic Center," Melody suggested. "The orchestra will be arriving."

"Yes, yes, of course," Victor responded absently, and drifted out of the room.

Melody hung back.

"You go ahead," Henry told her. "We'll stay here and straighten up."

Saying, "I'm sure Victor would appreciate that," Melody hurried off.

Benny and Soo Lee began putting things back in drawers. Jessie and Violet remade the bed. Henry put the clothes back on hangers.

"Now, we have two false notes," Jessie said.

"I'll bet they were both written by the same person," Benny said.

"But who?" asked Violet.

They thought about that.

Finally, Soo Lee asked, "Could it be Janet Muller?"

They remembered the scene in the hotel earlier that morning. Janet Muller had seemed uneasy. She said she was there collecting autographs. Had she lied?

"Maybe she is the one who wrote the notes," suggested Jessie.

"What about Melody's signature?" Violet asked.

"She could have traced it from her autograph book," Benny answered.

It was possible, they agreed.

"I'll bet she took the score, too," Benny said.

That made sense. She had been very interested in the score that first day. And Mozart's signature would be a valuable addition to her collection.

"But if she *has* the score, why would she need to search for it?" Henry asked.

"And if she didn't need to search for the score, why would she write the notes?" Jessie added.

Benny let out a loud breath. "We don't need more questions," he said. "We need answers."

But no one had any.

CHAPTER 12

The Audition

"I can't think about this mystery now," Violet said. "Tomorrow is the audition for the young people's orchestra. I have to go home and practice."

"We'll go home, too," Jessie suggested. "We can be your audience."

They trooped out of Victor's room to the elevator.

Outside the hotel, they were just in time to catch the bus.

When they were seated, Benny said, "This is a good idea — listening to Violet practice."

He turned to the others. "You know why?"

"Oh course we do, Benny," Henry replied. "Listening to good music is a wonderful experience."

"That's not the only reason," Benny said.

Jessie laughed. "Well, don't keep us in suspense, Benny. Tell us your reason."

"I might get an idea."

"Yes, listening to music often gives people ideas," Henry said.

"I mean about the mystery. I got the idea about the fake notes when Melody was playing. I might get an even better idea listening to Violet," said Benny.

But he didn't. The minute he and the others were seated around the living room and Violet began to play, Benny forgot about the mystery. So did everyone else. They thought only about the music Violet played and how proud they were of her.

"Now, I'll play 'Song of the Wind,'" she said.

The notes followed one after another, separate and clear and yet blended, like drops of water in a smoothly flowing river.

Violet played all their favorites, even "Twinkle, Twinkle, Little Star."

When she had finished, Jessie asked, "What will you play for the audition, Violet?"

Benny piped up, "Play 'Twinkle, Twinkle, Little Star.' I like that best."

Everyone laughed.

"I like them all best," Soo Lee said.

"I don't know which piece to play," Violet said. "I think I'll let Melody choose."

Benny got to his feet. "Now that that's settled," he announced, "I'm hungry. It's time for lunch."

Jessie put out sandwich fixings. That way, each of the Aldens could make his or her favorite.

Afterward, Benny raided the garbage.

"I'm going to use this cardboard tube to make a kazoo," he said. He placed waxed paper over one end and secured it with a rubber band. Then, he hummed into it. He liked the sound it made.

Soo Lee decided to make an instrument, too. She found several different-sized bottles and arranged them according to size. When she blew across the tops, she played a melody.

All afternoon, Soo Lee and Benny kept making instruments until they had enough for all the Aldens. When Grandfather came home from the mill, they gave him a concert.

"Bravo!" he said as they took their final bows. "You sound like a real orchestra."

"Part of what you heard was my stomach growling," Benny told him. He was hungry again!

After dinner, Grandfather asked Violet to play. She sounded even better than she had that afternoon.

"Violet, if you play like that, you're sure to win a place in the young people's orchestra," Grandfather assured her.

"Then we'll celebrate," Benny said.

Grandfather nodded. "Yes, of course, we must do that. I'll tell you what: You meet me at the hotel tomorrow afternoon and I'll treat you to dinner in the dining room."

"What if I'm not chosen?" Violet asked.

"You will be," Soo Lee responded.

Violet wanted to believe that, but she had her doubts. The competition would be stiff. She went to bed vowing to do her very best. "Then, whatever happens will be all right," she told herself.

The next morning, they arrived at the Civic Center to find the auditorium nearly full and buzzing with excitement.

Melody called for attention. "Will the musicians please come up to the front rows," she instructed.

Violet made a *this-is-it* face. The others wished her good luck, and she started up the aisle.

When everyone was assembled, Melody divided them according to their instruments. The strings would be first to play.

Violet was third. On stage, she carefully took her violin from its case. She put it in position and pulled the bow across the strings to be sure it was in tune. Then, she readjusted it, took a deep breath, and played the pieces Melody had selected from her list.

After the first few notes, Henry, Jessie, Benny, and Soo Lee relaxed. There was no question about it: Violet was very good and getting better all the time.

The orchestra list was posted in the reception hall at noon. There were so many people crowded around the bulletin board, it was difficult to see. Benny squeezed to the front of the group where he stood on tiptoe to read the list. At the very top of the strings section was Violet's name.

"Hooray!" Benny exclaimed. He squeezed back through the crush of people. "You made it!" he said, and hugged his sister.

Violet skipped off to call Grandfather. While the other Aldens waited for her, Henry picked up a printed concert schedule.

"When is the young people's rehearsal?" Jessie asked him.

"Tomorrow morning. Their concert will be Saturday afternoon."

"What about the regular orchestra?" Benny wanted to know. "When do they play?"

"Friday night."

"That's tomorrow!" Soo Lee said.

Benny sighed. "That doesn't give us much time."

They all knew he was thinking about solving the mystery. Could the Boxcar Children find the missing score in time for it to be displayed before the concert?

CHAPTER 13

The Plane Ticket

The Aldens took their sack lunches and went outside to the park beside the Civic Center. Jessie spread the blue tablecloth from their boxcar days on a grassy hillock. Benny had even remembered to bring his old cracked pink cup.

"This is like old times," Henry said. "All we need is the boxcar."

"And Watch," Jessie added.

"Sometimes I wish we were still living in the boxcar," Benny put in.

"I don't," Violet said. "I never would have

learned to play the violin if we hadn't come to live with Grandfather."

"And you wouldn't know me," Soo Lee said.

"That's right," Benny said to his sister and his cousin. "I forgot."

Henry laughed. "Things work out."

"Except for *this* mystery," Jessie said. "I wonder if it'll work out at all."

"Let's go over what we know," Henry suggested.

"We know the music's missing," Soo Lee responded.

"And that Victor took the score to the hotel," Violet said.

"Two false notes," Jessie added. "And two ransacked rooms."

"Don't forget about Melody and that mysterious man," Benny put in.

Henry looked sad. "We always come back to Melody, don't we?"

"It's not Melody," Violet said. "Someone else signed her name to those notes."

"At least that's what we think," Jessie reminded her sister.

Benny's face lit up. "I got it: Melody signed the notes herself and just told us she didn't."

"That's a possibility," Henry agreed.

"But what about the ransacked rooms?" Violet asked.

"Yes," Soo Lee said. "Melody didn't do that. She was at the Civic Center with us."

Henry shrugged. "Maybe she has a partner."

"The mysterious man! I'll bet he messed up the rooms," Benny piped up.

Violet crushed her lunch sack and got to her feet. "Melody did not do any of this!" She stalked off toward the Center.

"Wait, Violet!" Benny called. "We didn't say she did it — only that she might have."

But Violet was already inside the building.

Benny's shoulders slumped. He didn't like to see Violet upset. "Now what?" he asked the others.

"Let's go and listen to the orchestra rehearse," Henry answered.

They found Violet in the front row and

sat down beside her. Victor was at the podium, his baton raised, ready to begin.

"Violet, I — " Benny began.

"Shhh!" she said.

Just as the music began, Bob Weldon hurried in a side door. He saw the Aldens and headed toward them.

When he reached Jessie, he whispered, "I wonder if you'd be kind enough to run an errand for me."

"Yes, of course," Jessie whispered back. "What is it?"

Bob motioned for her to follow him.

"Bob wants me to run an errand for him," she told the others. "I'll be back soon." She started up the aisle.

"I'll go with you," Benny offered. He crawled over Henry and hurried after his sister.

In the lobby, Bob told them, "I left my glasses in my room. They're in my briefcase on the desk. I'd get them myself, but I can't leave right now. Too busy."

"We'll be happy to get them for you," Jessie said.

"Thank you," Bob said. He gave Jessie his room key and hurried off.

Bob's briefcase was on the desk in his hotel room. Benny got to it first. Its latch was closed. Benny fiddled with it.

"Wait, Benny, let me do — !" Jessie said, but it was too late.

The briefcase fell to the floor, spilling its contents everywhere.

Benny stood looking at the mess. "Oops," he said.

"Oops is right," Jessie said.

Benny began picking up things. "Here're the glasses."

"Just pile the rest on the desk," Jessie instructed. "No sense putting the papers back in the briefcase. We won't get them in the right order."

They were ready to leave when Benny saw something under the desk chair. He knelt down and reached for it.

"It's a plane ticket," he said and sat back on his heels to examine it. He handed it to Jessie.

"You're right, it's a plane ticket," she said and set it on the desk.

"Where's it to?" Benny asked. "Doesn't it say Paris?"

Jessie glanced at the ticket. "Yes." She examined the ticket more closely.

"That's in France, isn't it?"

Jessie nodded. "And the ticket's for tomorrow afternoon." She looked puzzled.

"That's funny," Benny said. "The concert isn't until tomorrow night. Why would Bob leave before that?"

Jessie shook her head. "I don't know, Benny. Maybe he has to go on ahead to make arrangements for the next concert."

"But the orchestra's not going to Paris," Benny reminded her. "It's going to Cleveland!"

CHAPTER 14

The Mysterious Package

Back at the Civic Center, they found Bob in the lobby, talking to some of the orchestra members.

"Did you find my glasses?" he asked when he saw Jessie and Benny.

Jessie handed them to him. "The briefcase fell over," she said, "so we put everything on your desk."

Bob nodded, but Jessie was sure he hadn't heard her.

"Why didn't you ask him about the plane ticket?" Benny wanted to know.

"He's too busy now," Jessie answered. "And there are too many people around."

Henry came up behind them. "The orchestra took a break," he said. "Let's go back to the park."

"Wait till you hear what we found!" Benny exclaimed.

"Not here, Benny," Jessie warned him. She didn't want Bob to hear them discussing the plane ticket.

When the Aldens were all in the park, Benny said, "Bob has a plane ticket to Paris!"

"It's for tomorrow afternoon," Jessie added.

"I'll bet he's taking the missing music with him," Benny added.

"Bob Weldon?" Soo Lee asked.

Violet was surprised, too. "He can't be the thief!"

Until now, they hadn't even considered him a suspect.

"Let's think about this," suggested Henry. And they did.

After a while, Jessie said. "What about his room? It was ransacked just like Victor's."

"Are we sure about that?" Henry asked.

"That's right!" Violet said. "We didn't *see* his room."

"He could have lied about it to throw us off the track," Henry added.

Benny laughed. "We weren't even *on* the track!"

"Bob didn't know that," Henry reminded him.

"But what about the notes?" Violet asked. "Janet Muller could have traced Melody's signature from her autograph book. How would Bob have written it?"

Henry had an explanation. "Bob manages the orchestra; he probably has copies of all the musicians' signatures in his files."

This was an important development. They decided to tell Grandfather Alden about it.

"Let's go to the hotel and wait for him," Violet suggested. "He said he'd try to get there early. He wants to have dinner before the dining room gets too crowded."

On the way to the hotel, they continued their discussion.

"Bob could easily have taken the score from Victor's room," Jessie said.

"Anybody could have done that," Benny argued. "Victor never locks his door."

"But no one would be alarmed if they saw Bob in the room," Henry said. "It's his job to take care of the orchestra members."

"You know what I don't get?" Soo Lee said. "If Bob had the music, why did he mess up Victor's room?"

That was something no one understood.

They weren't at the hotel long when Victor, Bob, and Melody came in. They stood near the door discussing the next night's performance.

A desk clerk approached, carrying a large brown envelope. "Excuse me, Mr. Weldon," he said.

Bob snapped, "Can't you see I'm busy?" and waved him away.

The clerk backed off.

"Maybe I could help," Henry offered.

"Thank you," the man said. "Perhaps you could talk to Mr. Weldon." He held up the package. "He asked us to send this out, but we can't read his handwriting. All we can make out is *Paris, France*."

"Paris!" Benny repeated.

The Aldens looked at one another. They were all wondering the same thing: What was Bob Weldon sending to Paris?

The clerk handed the envelope to Henry and went behind the desk.

"Why are you sending something to Paris, Bob?" Benny asked, his voice loud with excitement.

Bob grabbed at the envelope. But it was too late. Benny spoke up again. "Why don't you just take it with you? You're going to Paris tomorrow."

Bob glared at Benny.

Melody's mouth dropped open.

Victor looked hard at Bob. "What's this about Paris?"

"I — uh — " Bob stammered. His eyes darted around as though he were looking for a place to hide.

"He has a plane ticket to Paris," Jessie said. She explained what she had found in Bob's room.

Victor nodded. "I see," he said. He seemed surprisingly calm. He turned to Bob. "Open that package, Bob. Let's see what's in it."

"It's nothing," Bob said. "A letter!"

"Bob," Victor repeated.

"Oh, all right. Here." Bob handed the envelope reluctantly to Victor. Then he sank to a nearby chair and put his head in his hands.

Victor turned the brown envelope over. Slowly, he tore the tab on the back. The envelope was open. Victor reached in carefully and pulled out . . . the missing Mozart score!

CHAPTER 15

Two Confessions

Everyone stared at Bob Weldon. They were too stunned to speak.

Finally, Victor said, "I thought you were up to something." He looked sad and disappointed. "But I can't figure out where you found the score. If *I* couldn't find it, and I'm the one who hid it . . ." His voice trailed off.

Bob let out a hollow laugh. "Believe me, it wasn't easy!" He got to his feet. "I didn't plan this," he said and began to pace. "You're the one who gave me the idea."

Victor boomed, "*I* gave you the idea? That's ridiculous!"

"Ridiculous? That's what I thought when you couldn't find the score. How could anyone — even you! — be *that* forgetful?"

"I have a lot on my mind," Victor mumbled in defense.

Bob ignored him. "I decided then to teach you a lesson. I would find the score and hide it."

"By sending it to Paris?" Benny asked.

"That idea came later. Why not take it and sell it? I thought. Serve everybody right. Who'd guess I did it? No one ever says thank you or notices anything else I do — unless something goes wrong. Then I get blamed."

"Oh, Bob," Melody said. "We couldn't get along without you." She reached out to touch his shoulder, but he shrugged her off.

"*You* may know that," he said to her. "Does anyone else? Does the *great* Victor Perrelli know it?"

Victor eased into a chair. "I know it," he murmured. "I just forget to say it."

"I contacted a dealer in Paris," Bob continued. "He offered me a lot of money. I'd be rich! Have an easy life. No more fetching and carrying for people who don't appreciate it."

"Where did you find the score?" Henry asked.

"I didn't. Not at first. I searched everywhere in Victor's room. Nothing."

"So you wrote the notes," Soo Lee said.

"Only one note — to Victor. I lied about receiving one myself."

"And your room wasn't ransacked," Violet concluded.

"I lied about that, too," Bob told her. "And then, Victor, you gave me your tuxedo to have cleaned."

Victor nodded. "Yes, I remember that."

"The score was in it!" Bob said.

"Yes, yes," Victor responded. "I remember now. I put it in the inside pocket."

"So there it was! I decided to mail it to the dealer. The sooner it was out of the country the better. Then, tomorrow, I'd follow." Bob sank into the chair beside Victor. "You musicians are so talented," he said. "And everybody appreciates what you do. I have only one talent: organization. A thankless job."

"But a necessary one," Victor told him.

Bob murmured, "This orchestra has been my whole life." He covered his face with his hands. "I am *so* sorry."

After a tense silence, Benny turned to Melody. "What I want to know," he said, "is who was that strange man you met in the town square, Melody?"

Melody's face reddened. She glanced at Victor, then looked away. "I — I — " She couldn't seem to find the words.

Victor came to her rescue. "I think I can explain that. Melody has been feeling somewhat unappreciated, too. Am I right, my dear?"

"Well, it's just that the schedule is so . . . hectic," Melody explained. "I never seem to have time to think. I've been afraid that my music would suffer because of the pressure."

"You play like an angel," Victor assured her.

She smiled. "Thank you, Victor. Perhaps it's just performance jitters."

"But who was that strange man?" Benny asked again.

"He conducts another orchestra — one that tours less. He offered me a job," Melody explained. "I met him to give him my résumé. He gave me information about his orchestra."

"Is that all?" Benny said.

Melody chuckled. "Did you think the score was in that envelope, Benny?"

Benny was embarrassed. He didn't want Melody to know that he had suspected her. He opened his mouth to explain but nothing came out.

Violet spoke up. "Soo Lee and I never thought you had stolen the score, Melody."

"Violet's right," Soo Lee agreed. Then she asked, "Are you going to take the job, Melody?"

"That is the most important question I've heard today," Victor said. He took a step toward Melody. "Don't keep an old man waiting. What is your answer?"

Melody laughed. "Oh, Victor, you know the answer. How could I leave you and the orchestra?"

"What about all the touring?" Henry wanted to know.

"Well, if we didn't tour, I never would have come to Greenfield," Melody said. "And, most important, I never would have met the Aldens."

Victor hugged her. He and Melody laughed and cried at the same time. Then they hugged the Aldens. Before long, the tears were gone and only the laughter remained.

Suddenly, Benny noticed that Bob Weldon was heading for the elevators. "Bob's leaving!" he said urgently.

"Let him go," Victor said.

"But aren't you going to call the police?"

Victor shook his head. "Bob has made his own punishment. He will no longer be with the orchestra."

"And word spreads fast among musicians," Melody added. "He will never work with another orchestra."

Just then, Mr. Alden came into the lobby. Smiling broadly, he shook hands with Victor and Melody. To his grandchildren, he said, "I'm sorry I'm late. I couldn't get away from the mill. I hope you haven't been bored waiting."

The Aldens, Victor, and Melody smiled at each other.

"We kept busy," Henry told him.

"That's my grandchildren, all right," Mr. Alden responded proudly. "They never waste a minute." Then, he invited Victor and Melody to have dinner with them.

"I'd like that," Victor said. "I am very hungry."

"Me, too," agreed Benny, and he led the parade into the dining room.

CHAPTER 16

The Sounds of Music

Violet awoke early. By the time her family came down for breakfast, she had poured juice and made coffee for Grandfather.

"I wish I could be there for your rehearsal," Mr. Alden told her, "but I have to work this morning."

Violet was relieved. Having Mr. Alden in the audience during rehearsal might make her more nervous than she already was. "That's all right, Grandfather," she said. "You'll hear us play at the concert."

He finished his coffee and toast. "Good luck then," he said and started out. At the door, he turned back. "And the rest of you, no more mysteries. Hear? You've solved enough for one week."

They knew Grandfather was teasing. Last night, after they had told him all that had happened, he said, "You children attract mysteries the way a magnet attracts iron." But they knew he was proud of them for having solved this latest puzzle.

The Aldens joined the stream of young people flowing into the auditorium. Inside, Melody was directing them to their places on stage. Excitement filled the air.

Violet didn't seem at all nervous as she took her seat. She smiled to the string players near her and took out her violin.

One by one, the young musicians began to tune their instruments. Before long, the theater was vibrating with sound.

Benny put his hands over his ears. "It's hard to believe they can sound so good later when they sound so awful now," he said.

"I like to hear them tune their instruments," said Jessie.

Henry agreed. "It's exciting. It gets me ready to listen."

"I'm already ready," Benny said.

The first attempts were not good. Melody stopped the orchestra every few bars.

"Keep together," she instructed gently.

Time and time again they started and stopped. Finally, they made it through an entire piece. After that, it seemed to get easier and sound better. By lunchtime they had played the entire program.

"Not bad for a first run-through," Melody said. She told them to return late in the afternoon. Then, she dismissed them.

Early that afternoon, the adult orchestra held their final rehearsal. Later, it was the young people's turn once again. Then, it was home to prepare for the big concert.

"I've never been to a real concert before," Benny said. "I don't know what to wear."

"Your party best," Jessie told him.

Mr. Alden was the last one downstairs. He wore a tuxedo and a stiff white shirt.

"You look very handsome," Violet told him.

He smiled. "It seems to run in the family," he said as he admired his grandchildren.

The Aldens had front row seats. As the auditorium filled, Benny kept looking around.

"There won't be a seat left," he said.

"You're right," Grandfather told him. "The house is sold out."

The orchestra filed in and took their places. The audience hushed. Finally, the great Victor Perrelli entered. Everyone clapped. Victor bowed, then turned his back to the audience. He tapped for attention, paused, and raised his baton. Every eye was on him, waiting expectantly.

"Start the music," Benny whispered.

With a sharp downbeat, Victor did just that. The orchestra came to life. Victor swayed to the music, pointing to one section and then another. His baton was a magic wand, making all the different instruments sound beautiful together.

At intermission, the Aldens went out to the lobby. Mr. Alden stopped to visit with some old friends. The children went over to the display case to look at the Mozart score.

"Mozart's music is so beautiful," Violet said.

Janet Muller came up beside them. "I see the score is back." She looked around as if to be sure no one was listening. Then, she leaned in close. "Do you know who took it?"

Jessie was about to answer when Victor came into the lobby. Seeing the children, he hurried over.

Janet's hands fluttered nervously. "Oh, my. Oh, dear," she said. "There's the maestro." She stepped away as Victor approached.

It was nervous behavior like this that had made the Aldens suspect she was the thief.

"I haven't had the chance to thank you for all you've done this week," Victor told the Aldens.

"We were happy to help," Henry said.

"We like solving mysteries," Benny piped up.

Victor laughed. "You're very good at it."

Benny waved that away. "We've had lots of practice," he said.

Still laughing, Victor drifted off. Awestruck, Janet watched him go. "What a talented man," she said. "I have to go sit down — being around great stars like him makes me a bit light-headed."

The last mystery was solved. Janet wasn't nervous because she wasn't hiding anything. She was just starstruck.

The second half of the concert was even better than the first. Melody's solo was a showstopper. At the end of the performance, the audience rewarded the orchestra with ten full minutes of applause.

At the reception afterward, Victor looked sad.

"That was a wonderful performance," Mr. Alden said to him. "You should be very proud."

"The orchestra played flawlessly," Victor responded. "The praise is theirs. I'm just sorry Bob couldn't be here."

It was clear that Bob Weldon was not the

only one who would suffer because of his actions.

The Aldens left the reception early so that Violet could get a good night's rest. But she had trouble sleeping. Long after the others were in bed, the sweet strains of violin music drifted through the house.

In the morning, Benny brought his bear down to breakfast. Made from old stockings, it had been with him since their boxcar days. "I thought you might like to take Stockings, Violet. For luck." He held out the bear to his sister.

Violet was pleased. "Oh, Benny," she said, "that is so nice. But there's no place to put him onstage."

Benny wasn't the least bit disappointed. He had already thought about that. "You could put him in your violin case."

"But our instrument cases will be in a room offstage."

"That's okay," Benny assured her. "It'll still work."

* * *

Soo Lee and her parents, Joe and Alice, were waiting in the lobby. One by one, the Aldens gave Violet a hug and wished her well.

Victor and Melody ushered the young musicians and their families into the auditorium.

"Come, children," Victor said, "and we will make beautiful music together."

Janet Muller rushed up to the door. She thrust an open book and a pen under Violet's nose. "Would you please give me your autograph, Violet?" she asked shyly.

Violet was surprised. "You don't want my signature," she said. "I'm nobody famous."

Janet said, "Who knows . . ."

Victor, Melody, and the Aldens chimed in, ". . . Maybe one day."

Violet smiled as she signed her name. After the *n* in Alden, she drew a graceful flourish.

NOW AVAILABLE!
THE BOXCAR CHILDREN DVD!

The first full-length animated feature based on Gertrude Chandler Warner's beloved children's novel!

Featuring an all-star cast of voice actors including Academy Award–winner J. K. Simmons (*Whiplash*), Academy Award–nominee Martin Sheen (*Apocalypse Now*), and Zachary Gordon (*Diary of a Wimpy Kid*), Joey King (*Fargo*), Mackenzie Foy (*The Twilight Saga: Breaking Dawn*), and Jadon Sand (*The LEGO Movie*)

Available for sale or download wherever DVDs are sold

Create everyday adventures with the
Boxcar Children Guide to Adventure!

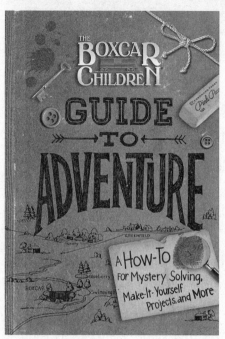

A fun compendium
filled with tips and
tricks from the Boxcar
Children—from making
invisible ink and secret
disguises, creating
secret codes, and
packing a suitcase
to taking the perfect
photo and enjoying the
great outdoors.

ISBN: 9780807509050, $12.99

Available wherever books are sold

THE BOXCAR CHILDREN
Fan Club

Join the Boxcar Fan Club!

Visit **boxcarchildren.com** and receive a free goodie
bag when you sign up. You'll receive occasional
newsletters and be eligible to win prizes
and more! Sign up today!

Don't Forget!

The Boxcar Children audiobooks are also available!
Find them at your local bookstore, or visit
oasisaudio.com for more information.

GERTRUDE CHANDLER WARNER discovered when she was teaching that many readers who like an exciting story could find no books that were both easy and fun to read. She decided to try to meet this need, and her first book, *The Boxcar Children*, quickly proved she had succeeded.

Miss Warner drew on her own experiences to write the mystery. As a child she spent hours watching trains go by on the tracks opposite her family home. She often dreamed about what it would be like to set up housekeeping in a caboose or freight car—the situation the Alden children find themselves in.

While the mystery element is central to each of Miss Warner's books, she never thought of them as strictly juvenile mysteries. She liked to stress the Aldens' independence and resourcefulness and their solid New England devotion to using up and making do. The Aldens go about most of their adventures with as little adult supervision as possible—something else that delights young readers.

Miss Warner lived in Putnam, Connecticut, until her death in 1979. During her lifetime, she received hundreds of letters from girls and boys telling her how much they liked her books.